4.76

Jimmy Yellow Hawk

Jimmy Yellow Hawk

by VIRGINIA DRIVING HAWK SNEVE

illustrated by OREN LYONS

HOLIDAY HOUSE ◆◆◆◆ NEW YORK

To my children,
who were my inspiration,
and to my husband
who gave me encouragement and assistance.

Author's Note

The names used in this book are actual family names of Indians on South Dakota Indian reservations. This story is fiction and as far as the author knows, none of the incidents in the story ever actually happened to any member of the families named in the book.

The Dakota Creek Reservation is a fictional place; however, as described in this book, it could be any one of the western South Dakota reservations.

Glossary of Sioux Words

DAKOTA: what the Sioux called themselves, meaning friendly people.

EÝAPAHA or EÝANPAHA (*á-yah-pa-ha*): crier, word carrier.

KIYUŚKA (*kye-yush-kaw*): set free.

SHA OR ŚA (*shaw*): red.

SÍCA (*shee-cha*): bad.

WAKANTANKA (*wah-kanh-tanh-kaw*): Great Spirit, God.

WASICU or WAŚICUN (*wah-shee-choo*): white man.

WAŚTE (*wash-tay*): good.

Contents

1

Little Jim

"Hey, Sha Sha!" called Little Jim as he saw his classmate slowly riding his pony down the lane toward him. "Hurry up! I have to be at school early today."

Little Jim's full name was James Henry Yellow Hawk but everyone called him Little Jim because his father was called Big Jim. Little Jim didn't like his nickname since he didn't think of himself as a little kid anymore. After all, he and his friend, Sha Sha Blue Dog were ten and in the fourth grade at the Red Butte Day School on the Dakota Creek Reservation.

"What's the big rush?" asked Sha Sha sleepily, making no attempt to hurry his pony. "I thought you could hardly wait for school to close for summer vacation. So, how come you want to get there early?"

"I have to tell Miss Red Owl that Dad said it's okay to have the picnic and rodeo at our place," answered Little Jim and urged his pony into a brisk trot. They were still two miles from school.

"Some rodeo, that'll be," said Sha Sha scornfully. "We'll get to ride calves and chase goats. Big deal!"

"You know we aren't big enough to ride real rodeo stock."

"I know *I'm* big enough, *Little* Jim," said Sha Sha.

"Oh shut up!" Little Jim answered angrily. "And hurry!"

He kicked his pony into a gallop leaving Sha Sha behind, but he could still hear him laughing.

It was bad enough when the other kids at school laughed and teased him about his name, but when his best friend did—well that made him feel almost bad enough to cry.

It was really only because of his name that Little Jim was glad school would be out soon. He was interested in most of the subjects he was learning although he hated arithmetic. He kept trying to do better in that subject because Big Jim said it was important to have a good knowledge of math in order to run a successful ranch. But it was hard to work at something he didn't enjoy.

He liked the teacher, Miss Red Owl, the first Indian teacher the day school had ever had. She was one of the few Indians who had graduated from college and returned to the reservation to work with her people. Because she was Sioux she understood the children's shyness. She accepted, without trying to change, their Indian ways of not looking into an adult's eyes when speaking to them. The white teacher who was at the school before Miss Red Owl thought the children were rude and disrespectful when they wouldn't look at her when she spoke to them. She didn't understand that they believed it was rude to do so.

Miss Red Owl was pretty as well as friendly. She was always dressed in attractive, clean dresses and wore her hair long in the Indian way, but neatly tied back. Because she looked so nice, the children became neater and cleaner to please her. She did not insist that the children speak only English in school and even the shy little first graders liked school right away when she talked Sioux to them.

Little Jim enjoyed the classes he had in the school room where Miss Red Owl taught the thirty-six students in the first through the eighth grades. The school also housed a kitchen and dining room where Mrs. War Shield, the cook, fixed hearty hot lunches which many of the children did not receive at home. Once a month she had 'Indian Food Day.' Sometimes they had thick Sioux fried bread, rich corn soup, and tart choke-cherry pudding. Once in a while she made corn bread, pinto beans, or squash—favorite foods from other tribes. Little Jim was amazed how many of the vegetables served at white tables were of American Indian origin.

Mrs. War Shield's husband was the janitor who kept the building clean and the furnace running, and looked after the horses the students rode to school. The War Shields lived in a house on the school grounds, and Miss Red Owl lived in the teacher's house provided by the Bureau of Indian Affairs.

The school was three miles from Little Jim's house. Until he entered the third grade his father had taken him to school in their pickup truck. They would always stop at the Blue Dogs', who lived a mile down the road, and give Sha Sha a ride to school.

Sha Sha's real name was Vincent, but because he had almost red hair he was called Sha Sha. *Sha* means red in Sioux. Little Jim wished he had an Indian name, too.

When the two boys were nine their folks let them ride their ponies to school and Little Jim always stopped at Sha Sha's.

Now Little Jim's peevishness with Sha Sha seemed to spend itself as he galloped along in the clear upland air. He thought about the holding corral that Big Jim had built down by the creek for cattle going to market. It was there that the end of year picnic and rodeo would be held. This was a good place to have it and last year it had been a big success. Little Jim had been really proud that his family's place was chosen. Now he was hurrying to tell Miss Red Owl that they could use the corral again so that she could send notes home with all the children to let their parents know.

'Just two weeks of school left,' he thought as he rode into the school yard well ahead of Sha Sha. There was the janitor's pony grazing in the back yard set aside for ponies the kids rode to school. A couple of children, who lived close enough to walk to school, were already playing on the swings and they seemed to be the only early arrivals.

Little Jim was glad because he'd have time to talk to Miss Red Owl before class started, and yet not have to stay out in the yard where the others would tease him for talking to the teacher like a sissy.

Miss Red Owl was sitting at her desk. "Good morning, James," she said as he walked up to her.

She always called him James which he liked better than Little Jim, even though the others made fun of the name James, too.

"Good morning, Miss Red Owl," he answered, taking off his cowboy hat. "My dad says he'll be glad to have the picnic and rodeo at our place again."

"Oh, good," she said. "Your ranch is such a pretty place for a picnic and with that little corral already built, perfect for the rodeo. Be sure to tell your father thanks."

She smiled at Little Jim. "You really have a nice family, James."

"Yes," he agreed shyly, not wanting to sound as if he were bragging.

"Didn't your mother graduate from the boarding school?" Miss Red Owl asked.

"Yes," he answered, "and she used to work at the agency office before she got married."

"She must have been a good student," said Miss Red Owl.

"Well," said Little Jim, "she's always telling me how important school is. She said she couldn't have worked in the office if she hadn't graduated."

"Has she ever thought of going back to work?"

"I don't know. She helps my dad at the ranch and she always says she has had a big job raising her family."

"I'd forgotten," the teacher said, "that you have an older brother and sister."

"Yes," he answered. "My mom is real proud that they graduated from high school too."

"I'm sure she is," Miss Red Owl said. "What are they doing now?"

"My brother has one more year in the army and wants to go to college when he gets out. My sister got married and lives in California. Mama wishes she lived closer so that she could see the baby."

"Oh, you're an uncle. How does that make you feel?" she asked.

Little Jim shrugged, "I don't know. My sister's been gone

so long that I guess I think of my family as only the ones who live in the house now."

"Your great grandfather lives with you, too?"

"Yes," answered Little Jim, "Grandpa Yellow Hawk. You know, he's so old that he can remember real history."

"Is that right? I'd like to visit with him sometime."

Little Jim nodded, but he had his doubts about whether Grandpa would like to talk to Miss Red Owl. Grandpa had some funny ideas about young women who went off to school instead of getting married and raising a family.

Reservation Home

Little Jim's father was a rancher and although he was not as rich as Tom Russell, his white neighbor, he owned a lot of horses and cattle. Big Jim worked hard on the 160 acres he had inherited from his father. He also ranched the land owned by his grandfather, Henry Yellow Hawk, who lived with the family.

Big Jim had told his son that soon after the Sioux were moved to the reservation by the United States Army, the government divided most of the land among the Indians. Each Indian was allotted, or given, a quarter section which the agency people expected them to farm. The undivided areas of the reservation were then opened to white home-steaders.

Grandpa Yellow Hawk called the government's attempt to make farmers of the Indians *sica*, bad. The first reservation Indians knew only how to hunt for their food. They had been people of the buffalo. But now the buffalo and other wild game were gone. On the small plots of land they were given many starved because they could not learn to make crops grow on such poor land. Too often, Grandpa

said, there was not enough water and the soil was over-grown with stubborn prairie grass. Many Sioux sold their land cheaply to white men whose cattle grew fat on the grass.

The Yellow Hawks, and a few other Indians, learned to raise cattle and horses and were able to make a living from the land.

Big Jim had often told Little Jim that he had quit the reservation boarding school in the tenth grade because he had to stay at home to work the ranch after his father had been hurt by a fall from a horse. When his father died Big Jim was tied to the land for good. He did a man's work helping his mother and old grandfather run the place. But Big Jim wanted his children to finish their education so they could choose another way of life if they wanted to. Little Jim was pretty sure that he wanted to be a rancher like his father but Big Jim said he'd be a better rancher for being educated.

Over the years Big Jim had built on to the old house which the Bureau of Indian Affairs had erected for his grandfather. Now it was a home better than many of the houses of the other Indians on the reservation.

A great number of Indian homes were old and run down because their owners did not have the money to repair them. In the better homes, such as the Yellow Hawks', the government health people had put in an indoor bathroom and a kitchen sink with running water. Little Jim's mother often talked about how grateful she was because she didn't have to haul water from the well anymore when she washed clothes.

The Yellow Hawks even had lights that turned on with a switch since the Rural Electrification Administration had brought electric power lines to their area of the reservation. Sha Sha's house had electricity too, but the government would not install plumbing because they said the Blue Dogs' house was too old and run down.

Sha Sha bragged that the government was going to give his family a new house and that it would be better than Little Jim's house.

Little Jim asked his father why the Yellow Hawks couldn't get a new house, too. The government wasn't giving houses away, Big Jim explained, but they would build one on an Indian's land if his house was in bad shape like the Blue Dogs'. The Blue Dogs would have to pay for the house a little bit each month, and if they couldn't meet the payments they would lose their house.

Some of the other Indians said that the Yellow Hawks were trying to be *wasicus,* or white people. Little Jim knew this didn't bother his father, because Big Jim said he didn't have to live without the white man's conveniences or be afraid to work hard, just to prove he was a good Indian. It did bother Little Jim and when the kids teased him about his name they sometimes said mean things about his being a *wašicu* as well. Little Jim didn't understand why, because his great grandfather always told him to hold up his head because the Yellow Hawks were full-blooded Sioux.

Grandpa had also told Little Jim that his father, Little Jim's great great grandfather, had told him how the Indians used to live, free to roam and hunt wherever they wanted. Grandpa said the Indians had a very hard time learning to live by staying in one place.

Grandpa liked to tell stories about when he was young and Little Jim was always eager to hear about the old days when Grandpa used to ride all over the prairie on his pony and never see a fence. When he was a boy, Grandpa told Little Jim, he could ride and ride and never see another living thing except for sometimes an antelope, or a coyote, or prairie dogs.

Such wide open spaces so thinly settled were really hard for Little Jim to imagine. Now there were fences and roads on most of the reservation and if his father had to go to town he would drive his pickup truck to save time. It would take all day to get to town on horseback.

"I sorta wish I could have lived in the old days, like when Grandpa was little," he told his father. "Grandpa didn't have to go to school like I do."

Big Jim smiled, "There were different ways of learning things in those days," he told his son.

"Grandpa says that his grandfather was his teacher. He says he learned all he needed to know about living on the prairie and getting along with people. But, you know," Little Jim said in a puzzled way, "Grandpa never tells about how it was when he was a young man."

"Do you ask him about it?" Big Jim asked.

"Yes, but all he says is that it was a bad time. I guess it was when the Indians had to stay on the reservation and were starving. He doesn't look sad, but I think he feels sad."

"I think you're right," Big Jim agreed.

❖❖❖ 3 ❖❖❖

Rodeo

TODAY WAS the last day of school, but it wasn't really a school day. Today was the picnic and rodeo.

The holding corral was filled with stock. There were goats in one pen, calves in another, and two pigs in a third. The stock had been loaned by local ranchers, Big Jim among them. Mr. Russell, their white neighbor, had donated the prize stock which the winner of each event would get to keep.

Little Jim had been down at the corral since eight o'clock making last-minute preparations. The rodeo was to be at ten and the picnic afterwards.

The first to arrive was Sha Sha, riding his pony to let Little Jim know he was going to compete in the races.

"Hi, Little Jim," Sha Sha greeted him as he tied the pony to the corral. "Is this where the race horses should be?"

"Hi, Sha Sha," Little Jim answered. "Yeah, that's okay."

"Bet I win the race this year," bragged Sha Sha. "I've been running my pony every day."

"I hope I win the calf," said Little Jim.

"I don't want one of those," said Sha Sha. "We're leaving

for Pow Wows next week and nobody'd be around to take care of it."

Sha Sha and his whole family liked to go to all the Pow Wows during the summer. Sha Sha's father was a rancher too, but didn't work as hard as Big Jim did. Mr. Blue Dog's father had been a white man, but he had been raised by his Indian mother and given her family's name. Little Jim couldn't remember what Mr. Blue Dog's first name was. Even though Sha Sha's father was only half Indian no one used his white first name. Everyone always called him Blue Dog, which made Little Jim resent his nickname even more.

Blue Dog liked to dance Indian and entered all the contests at the Pow Wows. He was a good dancer and many times won money or prizes of beadwork or costumes in the Pow Wow dance contests. He and his family went as far away as the Wind River Reservation in Wyoming and to the Turtle Mountains in North Dakota to compete in the Pow Wows. The only trouble was that while he was gone in the summer his ranch work never got done.

"This year," said Sha Sha, "I'm going to enter some contests, too. My Grandma has made me new moccasins and leggings."

"Gee," said Little Jim enviously, "that'll be great!"

They saw Sha Sha's folks driving up in their pickup, and

behind them Miss Red Owl's funny little foreign car. Then came the cars of parents, relatives, and friends of the students all coming to watch the rodeo. They parked close to the corral so that they could watch from their cars.

"Hello, boys," greeted Miss Red Owl. "Where shall I put my potato salad?"

Both boys ran up to help.

"Over here on the table," answered Little Jim as he led her and Mrs. Blue Dog, who brought meat balls, to the long plank set on saw horses which he had helped Big Jim fix up the night before.

Now all the parents and relatives seemed to come at once, in busy confusion, tethering horses, parking cars, putting the food on the plank, and calling greetings to each other. But by ten o'clock everybody was settled and the rodeo began.

Both boys and girls were contestants in all events, closely supervised by the fathers, who were stationed in different parts of the corral.

Miss Red Owl had to yell over the noise to get everyone's attention for the first event.

"Contestants for the goat-tying please report to chute number one!" She made the announcements just as if she were the official master of ceremonies at the Rapid City rodeo.

"The goat-tying is a timed event," she explained, "in which the contestant will ride a horse out of a chute down to the goat which you can see in the center of the corral. The contestant will jump off his or her horse, grab the goat, flip it on its back and try to tie three of its legs together. The winner will be the one who does all of this in the shortest time."

There were cheers from the watching parents after her announcement.

"It looks easy," she went on, "but the goats put up a good fight and the goat will have to be securely tied or it might wiggle loose and the contestant will be disqualified."

There were some sympathetic groans from the crowd, but she continued her explanation.

"The older boys in the seventh and eighth grades will be first and they will have the biggest, strongest goat to tie. The girls will be next and their goat will be almost as big. The youngest students will have the smallest goat. The winners will each get a goat as a prize."

The first contestant rode out of the chute to the cheers of the spectators and the first event was underway. As Miss Red Owl had said, the goats put up a good fight and three of the older boys were disqualified, none of the girls made it, and only one proud first grader won a goat.

"All eyes on chute number two for the calf riding!"

Miss Red Owl announced after the goats had been led away.

"This event is limited to fourth graders and up," she said. "Most of our entrants are boys, but we have one brave eighth grade girl to give the boys some competition.

"The contestants will mount the calf in a chute just like a brahma bull is mounted in a grown-up rodeo. The gate will swing open and out will come the bucking calf with the rider hanging on for dear life.

"If the winner can ride the calf past the line marked in the corral he or she will get the calf as a prize. Watch them ride!"

This was the event Little Jim wanted to win. He'd feel pretty proud owning his own calf.

There were four entrants before him. They all got thrown from their calf before reaching the line. Now he felt his legs shaking as he lowered himself down on the calf's back. He'd sneaked rides on his father's calves many times, so he half knew what to expect; but this calf looked bigger then any he'd ever ridden before.

The gate opened and he clenched his legs tightly around the calf, hanging on to the rope tied around the calf's middle. A contestant was allowed to use both hands to hang on with and Little Jim used them.

The calf spun around in a circle and Little Jim couldn't tell which way it was going, until it was headed on a buck-

ing run back toward the chute. Dizzy, he was afraid he'd have to jump before the calf hit the chute, but it stopped short, and turning sharply around ran the other way.

Little Jim could hear the crowd yelling. He heard his father, who was in the corral, yell above the others, "Hang on! Hang on!"

As the calf jumped Little Jim was jolted from his tail bone all the way to the top of his head. He felt as if his head would snap right off his neck.

The yelling of the crowd changed to cheering and Little Jim knew he'd crossed the line. He could get off the calf now, but the darn critter kept jumping and Little Jim didn't dare loosen his hold.

He hit the ground with a loud whlump. Face down in the dirt, he lay where he had fallen, all the wind knocked out of him.

His father rushed over and Little Jim felt himself being lifted up by the arms.

"You okay, boy?" Big Jim asked anxiously.

Little Jim leaned heavily against his father as he tried to stand. He was glad to have Big Jim's strong arms supporting him because his legs felt like rubber. He couldn't get enough breath to breathe normally. It hurt when he attempted to talk and suddenly everything went black.

He found himself lying on a blanket in the shade outside

the corral where his mother had been watching the rodeo. He tried to sit up.

"No, you don't!" said Mama pushing him back down on the blanket. "You just stay right where you are till the rodeo's over."

Little Jim ached in every part of his body and was glad to lie back again.

"Did I win, Mama?" he asked.

"Yes, you did, you—cowboy, you," she smoothed down his hair as she answered and Little Jim knew she'd been scared when he'd blacked out.

"I'm okay, Mama," he said and then added very proudly, "Now I own my own calf!"

He had missed the greased pig contest—a free for all for students of any age. Two pigs were turned loose and all the kids tried to catch one and hang on to it.

Little Jim had come around in time to watch the pony race. He cheered and yelled for Sha Sha to win, but his friend fell behind at the last moment, and Martin Iron, a seventh grader, won.

After the race Sha Sha came to where Little Jim was sitting.

"Did you see how Martin edged me out?" Sha Sha said angrily. "Boy, he cheated and oughta be disqualified!"

Little Jim hadn't seen Sha Sha edged out and thought

Martin had won fairly. He didn't want to argue with Sha Sha so he only said, "I'm sorry you lost, Sha Sha."

To Little Jim's surprise, Sha Sha became even angrier.

"I deserved to win!" Sha Sha sounded like he was going to cry. "I suppose you think you're pretty great winning a calf. You were just lucky that you got a easy calf to ride!"

Sha Sha angrily stomped away.

Little Jim didn't know what to think. He'd been happy about winning the calf, but Sha Sha's words spoiled everything.

⋄⋄⋄ 4 ⋄⋄⋄

Red Butte

SCHOOL WAS OUT and Little Jim was glad because now no one teased him about his name. But he was sad too, because Sha Sha had gone with his family to all the summer Pow Wows and he wouldn't have any one to hang around with.

He knew that Big Jim realized how he felt because he was permitted to do more of the ranch work. Last summer he had helped his mother around the house and fed her chickens and gathered eggs, but he had never helped Big Jim with the ranch chores.

Now Big Jim let him ride in the pickup to check fence lines, or they rode their horses to look for strays where the pickup couldn't go. But best of all Little Jim was allowed to ride his pony alone to look for strays.

He had a good pony which Big Jim had trained well. When Little Jim had to get off to check a ravine or a place the pony couldn't go, all he had to do was drop the reins over the pony's head and the animal would wait patiently until he came back.

Little Jim, on his pony, checked the hills and along the creek. He liked best to ride up on the Red Butte which was partly on Big Jim's ranch and partly on the neighboring ranch of Tom Russell.

The butte was a high flat-topped hill that rose out of the level prairie as if some big hand under the ground had pushed it up. Little Jim's Grandpa told stories about how in the old days the young men of the tribe would go to the top of the butte and pray to the great *Wakantanka* for a spirit to guide them the rest of their lives.

When Little Jim rode the narrow zig-zag trail up the side to the top of the butte, he knew he was riding over a path made by Indian braves of long ago. He'd get a scary, spooky feeling when he had to go to the top of the butte to look for cattle or horses which sometimes strayed there.

One afternoon Little Jim was sent up to the butte to look for a stray mare who would soon be having a colt. It was a hot day and there were thunderheads in the west. Big Jim told him to hurry so he would not be caught on the top of the butte when the storm came.

Little Jim's pony seemed nervous and jumpy as they started up the trail. He even shied at a gopher which ran across the path. Little Jim talked quietly to the pony, trying to comfort the animal with gentle pats.

They were almost at the top when the pony whinnied in fright, reared on his hind legs and attempted to turn around on the narrow trail. Little Jim stayed on the horse and tried

to calm him, but the pony refused to go on. Little Jim saw the storm clouds hanging low, almost overhead. He was afraid. Then he became angry at the pony because he knew he had to hurry to find the mare.

He got off the pony and tried to lead him, but the pony pulled back on the reins and balked.

Little Jim was almost crying, "Come on, boy," he urged, "we've got to hurry!"

Angry and frustrated because the pony had never acted this way before, the boy was raising the ends of the reins to whip the animal when he heard a rattle behind him.

Little Jim froze on the trail and so did the pony. He slowly let go of the reins and the pony obediently dropped his head and stood still as he had been trained to do. Slowly Little Jim turned around and saw, about three feet from him, a rattle snake coiled, with tail rattling and head swaying.

Little Jim didn't know what to do. His throat tightened and he swallowed painfully. His heart pounded like a Pow Wow drum in his chest. He had nothing to throw at the rattler and if he moved to pick up a rock, the snake might strike.

Suddenly, blue blinding fire seemed to crackle on the butte top. There was a loud boom of thunder that made his ears hurt as its echo rolled out over the prairie. When he could see again, the snake was gone.

The storm was upon them and he knew he had to get down from this high place where the lightning struck. He also knew that the mare might be somewhere on the top. Maybe she had already given birth to her colt, and both of them were in danger.

He decided to go on up, have a quick look and then hurry down. He mounted the pony, which was now docile and obedient, although his ears twitched nervously when it thundered.

They began the last climb up the trail when the wind and the rain came in great blasting sheets that made it hard to see. Then the pony gave a small whicker of greeting and his ears perked forward. Through the rain mist Little Jim saw a tall, pale form coming towards him. Frightened, he reined in the pony, thinking that he was seeing the ghost of a long dead brave.

"Turn around, boy! We gotta get off this high place!" It was Tom Russell riding his white horse.

Wordlessly Little Jim turned the pony, even though his heart was pounding so hard he was sure Mr. Russell could hear it.

The trail down was slippery, but the sure-footed horses brought them safely to the bottom of the butte. Mr. Russell led Little Jim to a shallow cave in the side of the butte. It was then that the boy saw that Mr. Russell was leading their mare, still big with her unborn colt.

The man, boy, and horses took shelter in the cave and waited for the storm to pass. They didn't talk because the thunder was so loud and constant that they couldn't hear one another. Great flashes of lightning seemed to dance down from the butte top.

Finally the storm passed. The sun shone low in the west and there was a perfect, brightly colored rainbow arching over the butte.

Mr. Russell and Little Jim left their shelter and stood for a moment enjoying the beauty of the rainbow and the sparkling, golden freshness of the prairie.

"Come, I'll see you home," said Mr. Russell. "I bet your folks are mighty worried about you."

They rode out over the prairie, slowly because of the mare. The whole prairie around came alive with the gay sound of the meadow larks. They seemed to be singing with gladness that the storm had passed and with thankfulness for the needed water.

They had not gone too far before they saw Big Jim riding hard through the wet grass. He sharply reined in his horse in front of them and smiled with relief.

"I need not have worried had I known my good neighbor

was watching over my son," he said as he shook Mr. Russell's hand.

"You have a brave boy, Jim," said Mr. Russell, "and here is your mare. I found her while looking for some of my strays. I'd say she was about ready to foal."

"We thank you, friend," answered Big Jim. "When the colt is born, it will be yours."

Mr. Russell smiled, but shook his head. "No, Jim. That is too valuable a gift to take, but thanks for the offer."

"But you have done my son and me a great favor," Big Jim insisted. "We want to thank you with more than words."

Mr. Russell thought a minute and then said, "Well, I have a Palomino mare, who could use the services of your golden stallion."

Big Jim nodded. "When the time comes bring your mare over."

They shook hands again. Mr. Russell also shook Little Jim's hand saying, "You're a brave boy to go up on the butte in a thunderstorm, but don't do it again."

5

Pow Wow

Little Jim was happy and busy helping his father, and the summer days passed quickly. Since the thunderstorm on the butte he kept an eye out for Mr. Russell's stock too whenever he rode out looking for strays.

Once a week all the Yellow Hawks got into the pickup and rode into the agency town. It was usually a Wednesday when the Tribal Land office was open, so that Big Jim could take care of any land business he might have. Also the cattle and horse buyers would be in town on that day and if Big Jim had any stock for sale he'd make arrangements with the buyers to come out to the ranch.

Little Jim rode in the back of the open pickup with Grandpa, who had an old car seat to sit on. It was usually hot and dusty in the back, and whenever it rained they would all have to crowd into the front. Big Jim hoped that he could make enough extra money this year to buy a proper car.

While Big Jim did his business, Mama went to the agency store and got groceries and the other supplies they needed. At the store there were always other women shopping and she liked to visit and catch up on all the news and gossip.

Grandpa usually sat on the long wooden bench in front of the store and visited with other old men there. He'd buy a bottle of pop that lasted all afternoon while he and his cronies sat and watched the activity in front of the store.

Little Jim sometimes went with his father to the office, but he usually got bored with all the business talk. More often he went with Mama and Grandpa. There was always a chance that if the store owner, Mr. Haycock, wasn't too busy he might give him a long stick of black licorice, for free.

He'd stand in the store, listening to his mother and her friends talk about who'd gotten married, who'd had babies, or who had died. He didn't think much of this woman-talk so he'd go out and sit with Grandpa and listen to the old men talk of the old days. It would be interesting for a while, but it seemed as if they always told the same old stories of when they used to break horses or were great hunters.

There were usually Indian boys his age around to play with and he was glad to see them if they didn't tease him about his name. They would play around the store, maybe hide and seek in the corners, or they might go over to the playground at the agency school and swing or zoom down the slide. Sometimes they'd wander over to the ball field and watch the white boys, whose parents worked at the agency, play ball. Little Jim would have liked to play too, but never thought to ask if he could, nor did the white boys ever invite him to join in their game.

After the office closed, Big Jim loaded the supplies and the family in the pickup. They all went to the new drive-in restaurant that had opened that summer. Little Jim thought this was the best part of the day because the whole family would have hamburgers and malts. After this they'd go straight home. It would be late when they got there and Big Jim had chores to do before it got dark.

On the last trip to town they had seen posters advertising the coming of the annual Dakota Reservation Pow Wow to be held at the agency grounds. Everybody in town was making plans to go and talking about the new clothes they were going to buy. Little Jim kept hoping that the Yellow Hawks would get some finery for the Pow Wow, too.

When he had about given up hope, he discovered Mama thumbing through the mail order catalog. But she wouldn't tell him what she was planning to order. Every day Little Jim rode out to the mailbox to meet the postal truck and make sure he got the package right away. When it finally came, he hurried the pony home, balancing the bulky package on his saddle.

The whole family gathered around the kitchen table while Mama slowly opened the package. Little Jim fidgeted while she untied the string and when he said, "Hurry up, Mama!" she answered calmly, "There's only one way to hurry, and that's to cut the string, and string is too hard to come by to do that." Finally all the knots were untied.

A bright new print dress for Mama was on top. She held it up for everyone to admire, and then unpacked a plaid shirt for Big Jim. They all could see that Big Jim was pleased, even though he only grinned and didn't say anything. Grandpa had a bright red shirt, and the whole family knew that he liked anything as long as it was red. Last to be unpacked was a cowboy shirt for Little Jim, and an unexpected surprise—new boots.

Grandpa put on his new red shirt and pretended he was a young man dancing at the Pow Wow. He sang an Indian song and danced around the table while Little Jim pounded the dishpan as if it were a drum.

Now that they had all their new clothes for the Pow Wow, the family began to get ready for the trip. Mama did a lot of cooking. She made fried bread and fried chicken and packed clothes and bedding.

Big Jim checked all his livestock and asked Mr. Russell to keep an eye on things while they were gone. Grandpa brushed his old high-crowned black hat and put a new feather in it while Little Jim polished his father's good boots and tried to help everybody.

When the day finally came, Little Jim and Grandpa crowded into the back of the pickup with all the bedding and the tent they were to sleep in for two nights.

It was afternoon when they arrived at the Pow Wow grounds and already many Indians were there camped in a great circle around the dancing place. There were all kinds of tents, even a few tipis, and an occasional trailer or pickup camper.

Grandpa grunted disapprovingly over the fancy campers. "Not like the old days," he grumbled. But Little Jim knew Grandpa was happy to be at the Pow Wow anyway.

They drove around the circle of parked vehicles until they found a camp site next to an old school friend of Mama's. The two women happily hugged and kissed each other while Big Jim started pitching the tent and Little Jim helped him.

Grandpa went off in search of old friends who sometimes sang for the dancers. Grandpa was too old to dance now, but he and his friends liked to watch and brag about how much better they had danced than the young people of today.

The first dance was to be held that evening so Mama hurried to get supper as soon as the tent was up. Little Jim dug a small pit in the ground and ringed it with fire stones which they had brought from home. He then laid the firewood which they had also brought with them. For many years the Pow Wow ground had been picked bare of any wood for camp fires. Some of the other Indians didn't bother with cooking fires anymore, especially if they went to a lot of Pow Wows; they used modern portable camp stoves.

Mama placed a metal grate over the stones, started the fire and put the big enamel pot of coffee on to cook. The pot would be there the whole time they were, always ready for anyone who dropped by to say *hau* and visit.

Mama also had an old black skillet and a kettle which she used over the open fire.

Soon the odor of coffee, frying meat and the smoke of other camp fires all blended into a smell which seemed to be special only to Pow Wows. There was a constant flow of people passing by. Some who knew the Yellow Hawks would stop to shake hands before going on. Others sat with them on the ground around the fire and had a cup of coffee and some of Mama's fried bread. When supper was ready, two men, friends of Big Jim, shared it with them. Grandpa was gone, probably having his supper at a friend's cook fire.

They had just finished and Mama was putting away the supper things when they heard the loud voice of the *eýapaha,* the official camp crier, calling in Sioux as he made his way through the camp circle.

"Dancers get ready!" he cried. "The time is soon!"

Now the people began to drift towards the dance ground, a circle of hard-packed dirt open to the skies. Around it was built a pine bough shelter for the spectators.

Mama threw her brightly colored shawl over her new dress and carried a blanket to sit on. As they neared the dance circle Big Jim went to one side while Mama went to the other where the women sat. Little Jim hesitated and then followed his father. Only little kids sat with the women.

As they looked for a place to sit, Little Jim saw Sha Sha all dressed up in his fancy new costume.

"Hey, Sha Sha!" he called.

Sha Sha looked around, saw Little Jim and waved. Little Jim ran up to him, glad to see his friend after so long. But Sha Sha turned his back as Little Jim approached, and walked away.

Little Jim stopped and slowly turned back to his father. He really felt bad that Sha Sha hadn't spoken to him, and wondered if he was still angry about losing the race at the rodeo.

They found a place under the pine boughs. There was much visiting back and forth among the men and a lot of loud joking in Sioux and English. Some of the men were passing a bottle around. Big Jim refused to drink, and when the other men teased him he said, "I'll leave the drinking to you young bucks. My money has to go for feed and a new bull."

Little Jim wandered through the gathering crowd toward the north side of the circle where there was an entrance for the dancers. To the left side of the entrance was the big Pow Wow drum with the singers seated around it.

He could hear the announcer calling out the names of the dancers and where they were from as each dancer entered the circle.

"Harry Little Bull: Cheyenne River, Two Moccasins: Ponca Creek."

Little Jim liked to hear the sound of the Indian names and he admired their costumes bright with feathers and beadwork. Some of the men had full headdresses, others a roach and some only a beaded band with a single feather.

The women and girls wore beautifully decorated deerskin dresses, or pretty silk ones with much beadwork. All either wore or carried brightly colored shawls with long fringes which swayed as they moved.

Both men and women wore moccasins, with or without leggings. Most had an anklet of bells which would tinkle to the beat of the drums.

There were many children dancing, some of them so little

that they had to hang on to their mothers' hands. Quite a few were Little Jim's age or older.

He heard the announcer say, "Blue Dog: Dakota Creek, and Sha Sha Blue Dog: Dakota Creek." He saw them enter and he waved. But Sha Sha, who looked very grand and important, didn't wave back.

The drum began its beat, the singers their high nasal chant, and the dancers began to move.

Oh, it was really something to see and hear! The women moved in a slow graceful circle while the men danced in and out among them. The men and boys were the fancy dancers, their bodies bending and swaying while their feet moved in patterns to the beat of the drum.

As the night came down, bright flood lights lit up the area and the dancers made weird shadows as they moved. Grandpa always grumbled about the lights. In the old days the people used to dance around a huge fire that burned all night.

Little Jim walked back to his father who was sitting cross-legged on the ground watching the dancers.

"Don't you want to go to your mother?" asked Big Jim.

"No! I'm not a little kid anymore."

"It will get cold," said Big Jim, "and she has a blanket to keep you warm."

Little Jim shook his head. This year he would stay

awake until the dance was finished and he would not have to be carried to their tent like a baby.

He sat and watched until the dancers with their bright colors and fast swirling shapes made him dizzy. He got up and walked back to the very outer circle where it was dark with only the reflected glimmer from the spot lights making huge dark shadow places.

Here he found boys his age pretending to dance.

"Hey, *Little* Jim," called one, saying "Little" in a mean way, "how come you aren't dancing?"

"How come you aren't?" he asked in reply.

The other boy laughed, "I could if I wanted to, but my brother gets to this year. It isn't because I'm too *little.*"

The others all laughed and Little Jim got the mad, crying feeling he used to get when they teased him at school.

As he walked away from them they called, "Hey, *Little* Jim, why don't you go sit with your mama."

He walked around in the dark, feeling miserable. He was glad to find Grandpa Yellow Hawk sitting by himself near the outer ring of the circle.

"Those bright lights are not good for the eyes," he said as Little Jim sat down next to him.

Grandpa put a comforting hand on Little Jim's knee, for he had heard the teasing, but he said nothing.

Time passed and Little Jim was getting sleepy and

cold despite his promise to himself to stay awake until the dance was over. Grandpa was dozing and Little Jim moved closer to him to keep warm.

He awoke to find Big Jim gently shaking his shoulder and realized that both he and Grandpa had been sleeping.

"Show your grandfather to the tent," Big Jim said quietly.

They helped Grandpa to his feet as he had gotten stiff from sitting on the cold ground.

The tent was dark and warm. After he had helped Grandpa to bed, Little Jim crawled into the bed of blankets his mother had made for him on the ground. 'Just for a minute,' he thought, 'just to get warm.'

The next thing he knew Big Jim was shaking him and saying, "Get up! It's going to rain."

The wind was making the tent flap and sway and flashes of lightning came followed by thunder.

He saw Mama and Grandpa piling the bed clothes in the center of the tent. He got up and helped them. He could hear Big Jim outside pounding the stakes more firmly into the ground so that the tent wouldn't pull loose and blow down on them. He could hear shouts and cries of alarm from the other campers.

He went out and helped his father dig a shallow trench all around the tent so that when the rain came the water would flow away from the tent and keep the floor dry.

All around them others were doing the same. Some were struggling with tents that the wind had already loosened. When the first drops of rain came, Little Jim wondered what Grandpa thought about those new campers now.

They crowded into the center of the tent, away from the sides, for to touch the tent made it leak. They were dry, and the wind had died, but the rain kept coming and none of them slept too well.

It seemed to Little Jim that he had just fallen asleep and then the morning sun was shining in his eyes. He went outside to find a soggy, muddy camp ground.

Mama was having trouble getting the breakfast fire started. All around people were drying out wet bedding. Some tents were down and their owners crawled stiffly out of cars or pickups where they had had to spend the night.

The Yellow Hawks, along with others who were not dancers, decided to go home. It would take all day for the ground to dry for the dancers, and besides, Big Jim was worried about storm damage at the ranch.

They loaded the pickup, putting the rain-heavy tent in last. Everyone but Little Jim was disappointed. He hated to miss the dances, but it wasn't much fun to be at a Pow Wow when his best friend wouldn't speak to him and other boys teased him.

⋄⋄⋄ 6 ⋄⋄⋄

Goes-Alone-In-The-Morning

AFTER THE Pow Wow storm there came a week of rain. The moisture was needed in the Dakota country, but there wasn't much for Little Jim to do in the house.

Little Jim liked his house and since his brother was gone he had a whole bed and a room to himself. This helped now that he had to be indoors. He read comic books, wrote a letter to his brother, and wished that his family had a television set like Mr. Russell's.

Grandpa had gone to visit an old friend who was sick and Little Jim really missed him. Grandpa always had a lot of stories to tell on rainy days. With so much time in which to do nothing Little Jim began to worry about his name. If he could get his family to stop calling him Little Jim maybe the kids would stop, too. He could hardly wait for Grandpa to come back so that he could ask him how to go about it.

The rains finally stopped and soon after, Grandpa came home. Little Jim helped him clean up his tent, for in the summer Grandpa put his tent up and lived in it until it got cold in the fall. Little Jim didn't understand why. Grandpa even slept on the ground though there was a soft bed for him in the house.

Grandpa had tried to explain. He said he stayed in the tent because outside, under the sky, he was *kiyuśka,* or 'set free' as he was in the old days.

He liked to visit Grandpa in his tent. In the evenings they would sit on an old horse hide on the ground in front of the tent and Grandpa would tell stories.

Grandpa always had to do certain things before he would tell a story. First, he would make sure that the small fire he had burning in front of the tent was burning well; then he would seat himself cross-legged at a distance close enough to the fire to give it a poke if needed, and yet far enough away so that he wouldn't get too warm. Sometimes when the mosquitoes got so bad that Little Jim couldn't sit still, Grandpa would put a small pile of sage weed on the fire.

At first the sage would smoke so badly that tears would come to Little Jim's eyes and he would start to cough. But soon the smoke cleared and the burning sage smelled good and sweet and drove the mosquitoes away.

The last thing Grandpa would do before starting a story would be to take out his bag of tobacco, pour a little into a small piece of white cigarette paper and roll a smoke.

Grandpa had an ancient red stone pipe that had been his grandfather's. He kept it in a very old leather pipe bag which his grandmother had decorated with colorful porcupine quills.

Little Jim knew that Grandpa used to let the pipe be used in the Sun Dance ceremony, but a drunken Indian had stolen it the last time it was used. The man had been caught before he could sell the pipe, but after that Grandpa refused to let it out of his possession.

Grandpa showed this special pipe to Little Jim but he never smoked it. It was a valuable pipe and many white men had offered much money for it, but Grandpa would never sell. Others wanted him to give it to the museum at the agency and once a man from the museum at the state capitol had asked for it. Grandpa always said no.

After Grandpa had lit his homemade cigarette, he would clear his throat a few times and begin a story.

On the first evening Grandpa was settled in his tent, Little Jim sat down on the horse hide and said,

"Grandpa, I don't like being called Little Jim anymore. How can I change my name?"

Grandpa cleared his throat and asked, "Why don't you want to be called Little Jim anymore?"

Little Jim was a bit embarrassed as he answered, "The

kids tease me about being a little kid, but I'm not little anymore."

Grandpa nodded in his wise way. "You think you deserve a more grown-up name."

"Yes," nodded Little Jim.

Grandpa puffed on his cigarette and cleared his throat again. "In the old days," he said, "there was an Indian boy your age who got a new name because of a brave thing he did.

"It was in the time of the long cold winter when there was more snow than any of the old people had ever known. The hunters had to go far to find game to kill. All the people had to eat was the corn the women had dried in the summer. Soon, that was almost gone. The people were starving and so one of the younger and stronger braves made the long trip to the government agency to see if the agency man would give him some food for the people. He returned with a bag of corn and nothing more.

"Soon after the young man returned he got sick. It was a coughing sickness he had caught from the agency people. Soon many of the Indians caught the sickness and the hunters became too weak even to try to kill a rabbit.

"There was a boy in the tribe who didn't get sick. His grandfather had taught him how to make snares to trap small animals. The boy had not been allowed to do any real trapping because the winter was so bad and his mother was afraid that he would get lost in a blizzard.

"When no one could go hunting, the boy decided by himself that he would go down along the creek and set some snares. Maybe he could trap an animal that they could eat. The boy did not tell anyone of his plan. He left the tipi in the morning while it was still dark and no one was awake.

"He went to the creek and then almost went home because it was so strange and different with the snow covering everything. He was scared, but he looked carefully along the bank and found tracks so he knew that animals were there. He set his snares and then went home before anyone found out that he had been gone.

"The next morning he again left before anyone was awake. He checked his snares and found that he had caught two rabbits. He was happy and ran back to his tipi with the rabbits. His family was very proud of him and his mother made a stew with the rabbits and the corn from the agency. The stew gave the needed strength to the hunters who were then able to go hunting again."

Grandpa paused to throw his homemade cigarette in the fire and give the fire a poke with his stick. He continued.

"The whole band was very proud of the brave boy and in the spring when all were well and healthy again, a council was called and a feast held to honor the boy.

"A deer was cooked for all the people and there was singing and dancing long into the night. At the end of the celebration the boy was given a new name. He was known as Goes-Alone-In-The-Morning and was not considered a little boy anymore, but as one who was growing to be a man."

Little Jim and Grandpa sat quietly after the story was finished. The fire was almost out and Grandpa gave it another poke with his stick, turning the wood, and it flared up again.

Little Jim stared into the flames as he thought about the story. He liked it very much and he wished he had lived in the old times so that he could do a brave thing and not be called Little Jim anymore.

The flames died down again and Grandpa grunted and stretched so that Little Jim knew it was time to go to bed. He said goodnight and went up to the house. That night he dreamed about Goes-Alone-In-The-Morning, but in his dream *he* was the brave boy.

The summer was almost over, school would soon be starting and still Little Jim hadn't thought of a thing to do about changing his name. One day he and his father were cleaning out the barn and hanging way up in a corner, Little Jim found some traps.

"Hey, Dad," he called, "what are these?"

Big Jim smiled as he took the traps, "Why, I'd forgotten about them. They're my traps. Tom Russell and I used to go trapping when we were boys—about your age. They sure are rusty."

Little Jim got all excited, "Do they still work, Dad?"

"Why, sure they will," answered Big Jim. "All they need is to be cleaned and oiled."

"Do you suppose I could use them?" eagerly asked Little Jim.

"I don't know why you couldn't," answered his father. "In fact I think trapping would be a good thing for you to learn."

Little Jim carefully took the traps down right away and started cleaning them.

"Whoa," said Big Jim. "You can't do any trapping till winter. Let's finish the barn first, then we'll work on the traps. There's a lot you'll have to learn about using them before you can trap this winter."

7

Jimmy Yellow Hawk

SCHOOL STARTED and on the first day Little Jim rode down to Sha Sha's. He wondered if Sha Sha would speak to him now. Sha Sha was waiting for him and was as friendly as if nothing had happened between them. They found they had much to tell each other about the summer.

Sha Sha had won some prizes and was very proud of himself. Little Jim was happy for him and forgot all about Sha Sha not speaking to him at the Pow Wow.

He told Sha Sha of his plan to do some trapping in the winter.

"Maybe I'll catch a wild bob cat or a wolf and get an Indian name for doing a brave thing," he told Sha Sha.

Sha Sha laughed, "Bob cats and wolves never get caught in traps, you dummy."

Little Jim was hurt. "Well, they might!" he said.

"Oh, all you'll probably get will be rabbits," teased Sha Sha.

Little Jim felt bad that his friend didn't think much of his plan, but he was still going to do it. He'd show Sha Sha!

64

That evening after school Little Jim told Grandpa of his plan to be a trapper. Grandpa was pleased that Little Jim was going to learn how to trap, but said it wouldn't be the same as Goes-Alone-In-The-Morning, because nobody in Little Jim's family was starving.

That made Little Jim feel confused about the whole thing. He asked if it would be a brave thing if he trapped a bob cat or wolf.

"You will be using traps for small animals," answered Grandpa. "Bob cats or wolves are usually too smart to get caught in such a trap."

"But could they?" insisted Little Jim.

"It is possible," answered Grandpa, "but if it did happen you would have to be very careful because they are danger-ous animals when trapped."

Grandpa went on to explain that there was bounty money offered by the state for wolves and bob cats because they were dangerous to the cattle. This made Little Jim very ex-cited.

"What kind of a name would I get if I did catch one of them?"

"That," answered Grandpa, "would depend on how hard a job it was and how much the bounty would be."

Grandpa smiled and went on, "You can trap rabbits.

Some people buy their pelts and they also make good stew."

Little Jim didn't think much of that idea. "I might be called Rabbit Boy if that's all I caught."

Big Jim went with him along the creek bottom and showed Little Jim the best places to set the traps.

"You must pick a sheltered spot," he explained to Little Jim, "out of the wind where the snow won't drift in."

Little Jim listened carefully because he wanted to learn all he could so that he could trap by himself and without his father's help.

"If an animal is caught in a trap," said Big Jim, "it is cruel to let it suffer in the trap."

He showed Little Jim how to use a club to kill the animals so that they wouldn't suffer. This was hard for Little Jim to do, and he asked his father why he couldn't shoot the animal instead, but Big Jim wouldn't let him take out a rifle by himself. If Little Jim ever did trap a bob cat he was to call his father to shoot it.

As soon as the first snows fell that winter, Little Jim took down his traps. After school, he rode his pony along the same places he'd checked for strays in the summer, but now the snow made it all look different. He set his traps in the sheltered places along the creek that he and Big Jim had picked earlier.

All the next day in school he had trouble sitting still. He

was so anxious to get home he didn't even wait for Sha Sha who yelled after him as he galloped out of the school yard. "Hey, what's your hurry?"

"Gotta check my traps," Little Jim yelled back.

"Get your rabbits you mean," laughed Sha Sha.

But Little Jim didn't care and he hurried home.

"Mama," he called as he rushed into the house, "I'm going to check my traps."

"Can't you say hello," Mama said. "Don't you want a cookie or something to eat before you go? It will be a while before supper."

"Oh, yeah, hi!" said Little Jim. He stuffed cookies in the pocket of his parka and picked up the gunnysack in which he would carry the animals home.

"Gotta hurry," he said, "see you later!"

His first day was disappointing for he didn't trap a thing. But he carefully checked all of the traps and went home positive that tomorrow he would trap something.

Little Jim worked hard all winter trapping. It never took him very long to check his lines because he rode his pony. He carried the gunnysack over his saddle to put the animals in. But, as people had said, all he ever caught were rabbits and he was becoming discouraged. Grandpa liked rabbit stew and thought it was a good thing for Little Jim to trap rabbits. Although no one called him Rabbit Boy, he was still

Little Jim and it seemed to him that a trapper should have a better name.

One evening after school, when he'd been trapping about two months, it was so bitterly cold and windy that Little Jim's mother didn't want him to go out to check his traps. But Little Jim was sure that he would have caught something important because he had noticed unusual tracks, different from a rabbit's, around his traps.

He bundled up in his parka and set out. The wind was blowing hard on his back as he rode and he was glad that he didn't have to ride into it. His first trap was empty, so he guided the pony on through the deep snow to the next trap. He had almost reached the brush where he had set it when he smelled the strong stink of skunk.

He reined in short. The pony danced around nervously and tried to turn towards home. Little Jim got off and walked up to the trap. It smelled so bad that he wanted to go home, too. But he remembered what his father had said about being cruel so he forced himself to walk, carefully, up to the trap.

The skunk was lying still in the trap and Little Jim let out the breath he had been holding. He was relieved that it was dead. He knelt down to release the animal, but as he reached for the trap the skunk suddenly moved and Little

Jim almost jumped into the icy creek. The pony gave a loud whinny of fright and took off for home. Little Jim ran after him.

Little Jim's eyes hurt worse than sage brush smoke had ever made them hurt. His nose and lungs seemed to burn and the awful, awful stink was everywhere.

Coughing and gagging, with tears streaming from his eyes, Little Jim ran behind the pony. He felt as if he were going to throw up.

Big Jim had finished chores in the barn and was in the yard when the pony came running through the gate. The pony had never come home alone before and Big Jim was worried about his son. He rushed into the house, grabbed his rifle and yelled, "I'm going out to look for Little Jim!" as he ran out the door.

He was about to mount the pony when he saw Little Jim floundering through the snow toward the gate.

Little Jim didn't even have to call out to his father because the skunk stink reached Big Jim before Little Jim did.

"Stop, right there!" Big Jim ordered.

Little Jim was trying awfully hard not to cry, especially as Grandpa had come outside too. Mama peeked out the door. Big Jim called to her, "Better get a bath ready, Marie. Little Jim will need one!"

Big Jim made his son walk in front of him back to where

the trapped skunk was. He had his rifle with him and from a safe distance he shot the skunk. He told Little Jim to release it and to tie it up high in a tree. In a few days they would come back and get it.

When they got home, Big Jim told his son to go out to the old shed behind the house where Mama and Grandpa had a tub of steaming hot water and soap waiting. Little Jim undressed and threw his clothes out the door. It sure was cold out in the shed, and the water was steaming hot, but despite his discomfort, Little Jim scrubbed himself all over. His mother wrapped him in a towel and a blanket and Big Jim carried him into the house where Grandpa had warm pajamas and a chair waiting by the stove.

Big Jim had to pile all of the boy's clothes in the back yard, pour kerosene over the pile and burn it because the skunk smell would never come out.

Little Jim, clean and not so smelly any more, was very unhappy. Neither Grandpa nor his father had scolded him, but he knew his mother was upset about the expensive new parka that had to be burned.

Mama made hot tea for him and coffee for everybody else. They all sat around the stove not saying anything and then Grandpa cleared his throat as he usually did before starting to tell a story.

The story, this time, was about an Indian boy who didn't

like his name and who wanted to change it because he thought he wasn't a little boy anymore. The boy had worked hard all winter learning to be a trapper and brought home many rabbits to make good stew. The boy had learned many things about trapping and his family was proud of him. The boy had learned in a very hard way that it wasn't necessary to trap a big dangerous animal, like a bob cat, to have trouble. This boy hadn't earned a great name as had the boy Goes-Alone-In-The-Morning, nor did Sioux boys of today usually earn Indian names for deeds of valor, in the old way.

Little Jim knew Grandpa was telling the story about him, but he said nothing.

Grandpa continued his story, "Now in the old way, this boy would have been given a name as a result of what had happened with the not so dangerous animal. Such a name might be Skunk Face and he would have to go by that name whether he liked it or not. When the people, in the old way, heard the name Skunk Face they would know right away how he had gotten his name."

Little Jim felt ashamed and hung his head, but Grandpa went on.

"In the old way the boy would have to work very hard to show the people that he had learned from his experience. He would have to learn that it is best to ride with the wind in one's face when approaching a trap. He would have learned that he should never get close to the trap until he was sure the animal was dead. Indian boys of today can learn these things also."

Grandpa turned to Little Jim and said, "I think the name Little Jim is now not right for you because you have learned many things as a trapper and provided your family with much good food this winter. But would you want to be named Skunk Face as in the old way?"

Little Jim was almost crying. He shook his head and said very quietly, "No, maybe I'd better stay Little Jim."

His father got up from his chair and came over to Little Jim, putting a hand on his shoulder and said, "When I was a boy I was called Jimmy. That is not as grand as Goes-Alone-In-the-Morning," and then he smiled, "or as fancy as Skunk Face, but it would show that you are growing up."

"But the other kids will still call me Little Jim," he answered, wiping tears away.

"That," said his father, "is something that is not important because you know and we know that you are not little anymore."

Little Jim nodded in agreement, but he really wasn't sure that he wouldn't still be bothered if the boys teased him.

Mama got up, taking the empty cups. "That's enough excitement for a day," she said, "it's time for our boy, no matter what his name is, to go to bed." She gave him a hug before he went to his room.

"I think Jimmy is a fine name for a big boy," said Mama.

During the rest of the winter, Big Jim went out more often to help his son. He taught Little Jim where to look for rabbits and how to identify their tracks and tell them apart from the spoor of skunks and other wild creatures who sometimes foraged near the creek.

Little Jim came to know the special hunting grounds of all the animals who visited the creek. One day he pleased his father by recognizing the tell-tale signs left behind by a muskrat who had been digging for roots near the bank. Big Jim said, "If there were still mink around, that muskrat would be lucky to last through the winter."

"But minks are too tiny to hunt muskrats, aren't they?" Little Jim wanted to know.

"Don't you believe it," his father said. "Minks are lethal. They'll strike at anything that moves. Remember, they belong to the weasel family—the deadliest animals for their size that we know."

Mama was waiting supper for them one evening and Little Jim came bursting into the house, so excited that he didn't make much sense.

Mama and Grandpa grabbed their coats and went outside to see what all the commotion was about.

Big Jim, smiling very proudly, was holding up a mink for them to see.

"See what our trapper got?"

Mama and Grandpa were very impressed. Mink had been rare in the area for a long time and for any one to trap one was unusual.

"Where did you get it, Lil—Jimmy?" asked Grandpa.

"In the same place I got the skunk," was the answer and they all laughed.

Big Jim helped skin and tan the pelt and then they took it to town. Big Jim was sure it would sell for enough money to buy a new parka.

The store was filled with people as they walked in. Sha Sha and his father were sitting on blocks of salt and greeted the Yellow Hawks warmly.

Big Jim placed the bag with the mink in it on the counter and took the pelt out when Mr. Haycock came over.

"Hey, a mink!" the storekeeper said. He picked it up and carefully examined it. "They've been mighty scarce for a long time."

He held it up for all in the store to see, "Looks like a prime one, too. Where'd you trap it?" he asked.

Big Jim turned and spoke loud enough for everyone to hear, "My son, *Jimmy,* trapped it!" he said and there was pride in his voice.

"You don't say," said Mr. Haycock. He reached over to shake Jimmy's hand. "Boy, you're growing up! Congratulations."

To the others in the store he announced, "Hey, look here, Jimmy Yellow Hawk trapped this mink all by himself! What do you think of that?"

There were murmurs of *waśte*, 'good,' as they crowded around to shake Jimmy's hand and admire the pelt.

Jimmy was very proud and happy. What pleased him most of all was that no one, not even Sha Sha, called him Little Jim anymore. He had become Jimmy to everyone.